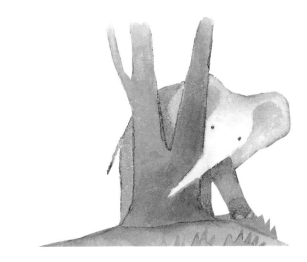

Little Elephant's Walk

Little Elephant's Walk

Adrienne Kennaway

Willa Perlman Books
An Imprint of HarperCollins*Publishers*

Little Elephant's Walk
Copyright © 1991 by Adrienne Kennaway
First published in Great Britain by Orchard Books,
96 Leonard Street, London EC2A 4RH

Printed in Belgium. For information address HarperCollins
Children's Books, a division of HarperCollins Publishers,
10 East 53rd Street, New York, NY 10022.
Typography by Al Cetta
1 2 3 4 5 6 7 8 9 10
First American Edition, 1992

Library of Congress Cataloging-in-Publication Data
Kennaway, Adrienne, date
 Little elephant's walk / Adrienne Kennaway.
   p.   cm.
 "A Willa Perlman book."
 Summary: Roaming over the plains and through the forests of
Africa, Little Elephant sees a lion, a giraffe, an aardvark, and many
other animals.
 ISBN 0-06-020377-3.—ISBN 0-06-020378-1 (lib. bdg.)
 1. Elephants—Juvenile fiction.   2. Animals—Juvenile fiction.
[1. Elephants—Fiction.   2. Animals—Fiction.   3. Africa—Fiction.]
I. Title.
PZ10.3.K33Li   1992   91-19727
[E]—dc20   CIP
                                                             AC

This is Little Elephant. He lives in Africa. All day
Little Elephant roams over the plains and through the
forests with his mother.

And as he walks, he sees animals....

As the sun comes up over the plain,
Little Elephant sees a lion stalking
through the long grasses.

The impalas see the lion too. They bound away so the lion will not catch them. But a herd of zebras continues grazing peacefully.

Down on the ground Little Elephant sees an elephant shrew. She will use her long nose to root for beetles.

A brightly colored agama lizard scuttles along with his mate, and a tortoise trundles by, munching.

A father ostrich stands nearby, shielding his chicks from the burning sun, while a hungry hyena sniffs around for bones.

A rhinoceros thunders past, snorting, with an egret riding on his back to keep insects away. Little Elephant and his mother get out of the way—but the rhinoceros won't hurt them.

The elephants stay away from the ratel, too. He is very fierce. A bird called a honey guide is leading him to a tree where there are bees making honey. Ratels love honey!

A cheetah streaks past at top speed,

while some patas monkeys sit in the sunshine, relaxing
with their baby.

In the heat of the midday sun Little
Elephant sits down near some strange-
looking mounds built from earth and
sand by insects called termites.

Nearby a bat-eared fox sniffs
hungrily at some dung beetles. They are busy
rolling a ball of dung into a hole.

A family of mongooses sit outside the empty termite mound where they live. They are on the lookout for snakes.

Meanwhile, a warthog kneels down to graze.

Then a crowned crane leaps into the air, honking noisily. He is dancing to attract a mate.

And here comes a pangolin, shooting out his sticky tongue to catch ants.

Little Elephant moves on to find some plants to eat, watched by a shy caracal and her baby.

Now the elephants stroll under a tree where a leopard is resting. He likes to lie along a branch, enjoying the cool breeze made by the leaves…

unlike the python, who likes to lie out in the hot sun,
coiled around some rocks. Nearby, a baby giraffe
nuzzles his mother.

A porcupine rattles her spines and
stamps her feet to frighten Little
Elephant away,

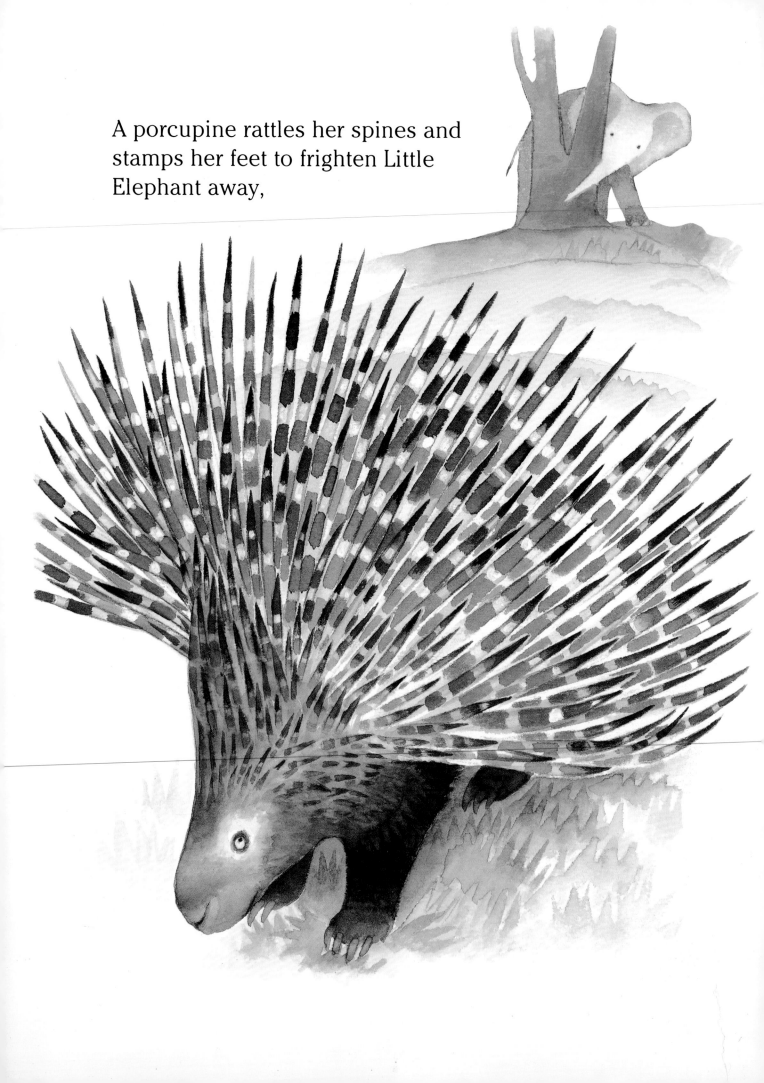

and a big fierce mandrill barks at him.

High up on a branch, a chameleon catches a fly with his long tongue. He has made himself the same color as the leaves so that he can't be seen.

A fruit bat cradles her baby in her folded wings,

and a mother baboon passes by, carrying her baby
on her back.

Deep in the forest, colobus monkeys
swing from tree to tree. They screech
and chatter at Little Elephant when
he stops to scratch himself
on a tree trunk.

Now Little Elephant wanders down to the river to splash himself with cool water, while hyraxes play about on the rocks above.

A mother hippopotamus walks along under the water with a baby riding high up on her back. A monitor lizard crawls out of the river, flicking his tongue. He is searching for birds' nests to rob.

Little Elephant has seen a crocodile!
He hides in the reeds so the crocodile
won't see him. The crocodile is
letting a plover clean his teeth
by picking the little pieces of
meat from between them.

Nearby, some vultures are busy smashing open an
ostrich egg to get at the goodness inside.

And an otter splashes in the water, playing games
with a fish she has caught.

As the sun sets and it grows dark, Little Elephant
hears rustling noises high up in the trees, where two
tiny bush babies are playing.

A slow, sleepy potto still clings to the branch where he has been resting all day. Close by, a genet—a kind of cat—stares at a grasshopper, waiting to snap him up.

Now it is night, and Little Elephant can see some of the animals that have been sleeping all day.

A mother aardwolf and her young creep out of their den to go hunting for food.

Some springhaas bound away, startled by the elephants, and an aardvark snuffles in the dark as he grubs for termites.

Little Elephant moves silently over the darkened plain, safe at his mother's side. He is sleepy now.

All around him animals are sleeping or awake…the animals of Africa that Little Elephant sees as he walks.